TARONGA

PRESENTS

POO AT THE ZOO

ALSO IN THIS SERIES

TARONGA

PRESENTS

PARTY ANIMALS

Sophia and Ollie are zookeepers for a day . . .
and it's a celebration at Taronga Western Plains Zoo!

BABY BOOM

Sophia and Ollie are zookeepers for a day . . .
and there are lots of new babies at the Zoo!

NIGHT OWLS

Sophia and Ollie are zookeepers for a day . . .
and a night!

TARONGA PRESENTS

POO AT THE ZOO

KRISTIN DARELL

Illustrated by LAURA WOOD

PENGUIN BOOKS

PENGUIN BOOKS

UK | USA | Canada | Ireland | Australia
India | New Zealand | South Africa | China

Penguin Random House Australia

Penguin Random House Australia is part of the Penguin Random House group of companies whose addresses can be found at global.penguinrandomhouse.com.

First published by Penguin Books,
an imprint of Penguin Random House Australia Pty Ltd, in 2024

Cover design by Caroline Lee © Penguin Random House Australia Pty Ltd
Author photography by Rebecca Erin Photography
Illustrator photography by Laura Wood

Printed and bound in Australia by Griffin Press, an accredited ISO AS/NZS 14001 Environmental Management Systems printer

NATIONAL LIBRARY OF AUSTRALIA

A catalogue record for this book is available from the National Library of Australia

FSC www.fsc.org MIX Paper | Supporting responsible forestry FSC® C018684

ISBN 978 1 76134 743 6 (Paperback)

penguin.com.au

We at Penguin Random House Australia acknowledge that Aboriginal and Torres Strait Islander peoples are the Traditional Custodians and the first storytellers of the lands on which we live and work. We honour Aboriginal and Torres Strait Islander peoples' continuous connection to Country, waters, skies and communities. We celebrate Aboriginal and Torres Strait Islander stories, traditions and living cultures; and we pay our respects to Elders past and present.

We proudly Acknowledge the Cammeraigal (Taronga Zoo, Sydney) and Wiradjuri (Taronga Western Plains Zoo, Dubbo) people, their Country, spirit and traditions as customary owners of the lands upon which our Zoos stand.

Chapter 1

A real job

'Ollie, come on,' Sophia yelled, waving goodbye to her dad, and racing towards the Taronga Zoo entrance. She barely paused as she bounded up the steps two at a time and then ran under the archway.

As she flew down the stairs and around the corner, the sound of traffic was replaced by the tweets, chirps, squeaks, warbles and caws of countless birds. It felt like entering another world –

a wildlife world. For Sophia, it felt like coming home.

A couple of kookaburras laughed as she charged past. One of them had wild ruffled feathers sticking up out of its head.

'Sorry to disturb you, kookas,' Sophia said. She paused near the ticket office to see where Ollie was.

She couldn't stop the giggle that burst out as her best friend jogged towards her, sandy-coloured curls sticking in all directions. His hat must have fallen off during his dash from the car park.

He looked just like the ruffled kookaburra!

Ollie was clutching his hat in one hand, along with his water bottle. He had a notebook and pen in his other hand.

'Did you sleep in *again*?' she said.

Ollie put everything on the ground, shrugged off his backpack and packed it.

'Why are we in such a hurry?' he asked.

'Because,' Sophia said, bouncing on her toes, 'today is THE DAY.'

'Okaaaaay . . .' Ollie stood back up. 'Let me guess. It's Monday?'

Sophia put a hand on her hip and squeezed her lips together. Ollie's confused look only lasted a second before his mouth turned up into a grin.

'You should see your face,' he said. 'As if I don't know.'

Sophia huffed and snatched his water bottle, squirting cool water into her mouth.

'But, Soph,' Ollie continued, taking the bottle back, 'your mum said we had to meet her at eight o'clock. We've still got ten minutes. Plenty of time.'

'I want to be early. We're getting a real job at last. A zookeeper job. Something different – important – special. Just like Mum!'

Sophia's mum was one of the vets at Taronga's Wildlife Hospital and was so passionate that she even fostered orphaned native animals to hand raise them until they could be released into the wild.

'Can we go now?' Sophia asked.

'Sure. But no more running.'

'Fine. Walk fast.'

Sophia fell into step beside Ollie, as they headed along the entrance plaza, already filled with staff getting everything ready. Shouts of 'hello' and 'good luck' followed them as they passed. Ollie's dad worked at the zoo as well, so Sophia and

Ollie knew everyone and everyone knew them.

'Hey, Dad,' Ollie called out, spotting him up a ladder near the toilet block. Ollie's dad was in the Backyard Team. They did important practical jobs all over the Zoo and helped with things the animals needed.

'Hey, guys. Have fun today,' he called.

'We will,' Ollie said.

'What do you think our job's going to be?' Sophia asked, as they kept moving.

'Well, it's not with the Backyard Team,' Ollie said. 'Dad would have said something.'

'Do you think it could be in the Wildlife Hospital?' Sophia asked. 'Oooh, maybe we'll be working on the echidna breeding program.'

'Or helping train the seals.' Ollie's eyes were shining.

'Or . . .' Sophia turned to Ollie.

'LIONS!' they said together, grinning.

Sophia sighed. 'I'd seriously be happy to do anything with the lions. How awesome would that be?'

'The awesomest,' Ollie replied. 'Actually, is that even a word?'

'Hey, you two.' A familiar voice called from the gift shop.

'Pixie!' Sophia bolted over, almost knocking Pixie over with a full-body hug. 'I'm so glad you're here today.'

Pixie had been volunteering at the Zoo since she was thirteen as part of YATZ, the Youth at the Zoo Program. Now she was out of school, she was still volunteering, but also studying to be a zookeeper. Plus she had a part-time job in the gift shop.

With her pink hair and green eyes, she was the coolest person Sophia knew. Maybe now they'd even get to work together.

'I hear it's a big day for you guys,' Pixie said.

'What did you hear? Who did you talk to? Do you know what our job is?'

Pixie laughed at Sophia's rapid-fire questions.

'I might,' Pixie said, one side of her mouth quirking up. 'But you'll find out soon enough. You'd better get a move on.'

Sophia glanced at her watch.

'Crackers!' she said. 'Seven minutes. Come on, Ollie.'

Sophia pushed Ollie around the

corner, down the stairs, and straight through the ticket gates. They waved at the person setting up for the day.

Sophia or Ollie never needed a ticket. Having a parent working at Taronga was like having a permanent Zoo pass.

As they rounded the corner, they saw a crowd of little squirrel monkeys gathered on a branch near the edge of their habitat to greet them.

Their black noses, framed by little white faces, were twitching as they looked around.

'Morning, Inuki and Lorenzo! Hello, Yasuni and Nadal!' Sophia called to them, slowing to a walk. 'Where's Toto?'

'There he is,' Ollie said, waving furiously. 'Hi, everyone.'

As if in answer, they all started chattering excitedly.

'I hope we get to look after them,' Sophia said, as they hurriedly moved on. 'They're so cute.'

'We should say hi to Willow and Ella too,' Ollie said, pointing to gulamany nura, Koala Country.

Sophia laughed. 'GOOD MORNING, sleepyheads!' she yelled. 'You know they'll be asleep, like always.'

'Well, you'd sleep a lot too if all you ate was eucalyptus leaves,' Ollie said. 'They don't get much energy from that diet.'

'What's your excuse for sleeping so much?' Sophia asked, raising her eyebrows.

Ollie grinned and shrugged. 'I just like it.'

As they walked up the path to the Taronga Institute of Science and Learning, they saw Sophia's mum step through the doors.

Sophia gave her a quick hug.

'Hi, Donna,' Ollie said.

'Good morning! Right on time.'

Sophia glanced at Ollie. He smiled.

'Come on then,' Donna said. 'It's time to get to work.'

Sophia's heart was pounding as she followed her mum into the building.

One day she hoped to be walking through these doors to start her animal care training and eventually as a wildlife vet. This job was the start, and it was going to be so special. She could feel it.

Chapter 2

Poo!

'Poo?' Sophia's eyebrows were pushing her forehead into more creases than Esmeralda's neck – and Esmeralda was an Aldabra giant tortoise, more than a hundred years old.

'Yes, poo,' her mum said, a smile playing at the corners of her mouth.

She might be finding it funny, but Sophia wasn't. She could feel the hot prickle of tears in the back of her eyes.

She'd imagined so many things, but she'd never thought their first official volunteer job would be picking up poo. She fought to hold it together.

'It's just . . .' Ollie started, eyes flicking from Donna to Sophia and back. 'Well, it's just not . . .' He looked down, his feet fidgeting on the polished concrete floor.

'I want you to keep an open mind,' Donna said. 'Look at me.' She waited until they did. 'This is a very special opportunity. I promise.' She smiled, then turned as a tall lady with bouncing curls jogged towards them. It was Kim. Head of the YATZ volunteers.

'How are my new trainees feeling this morning?' she asked.

'Good thanks, Kim,' Sophia said.

She looked at Ollie. He was unusually

quiet and seemed a little pale.

'Just you wait. Poo patrol is the best,' Kim said. 'Come on. This way.'

'Off you go,' Sophia's mum said, shooing them away. 'I'll see you later.'

Kim paused at a locked door. Sophia knew behind it were fun education rooms, but also special animal habitats.

Kim tapped her access card and let them through, guiding them to one of the shaded bench seats.

'Only trained volunteers are allowed to have an access card,' she said. 'That means they can come and go around here on their own. They've never been given to kids.' Kim's face was now serious. 'But, if you both work hard and prove yourselves over the next two weeks, then you two will become our youngest-ever official volunteers.'

Kim produced two Taronga lanyards and held them out.

Sophia glanced at them and then it hit her. This was a test. Her eyes darted to Ollie. He still looked like he'd rather not be there. She knew how easily he got grossed out - he was always trying to get out of helping with his little sister, Katy's, nappies.

'These are just visitor passes,' Kim said. 'But I hope they'll be more soon.'

Now Ollie did look up, his face still pale and sad.

'But poo?' he said. 'We thought –'

'Thanks so much, Kim,' Sophia interrupted quickly. 'We won't let you down. Being real volunteers would be a dream come true.'

Ollie stared at her as she took her pass.

'Whatever it takes,' Sophia said, looking straight at Ollie.

Suddenly, he seemed to catch on. He sat up straighter.

'Right,' he said, taking his lanyard and squaring his shoulders. 'Thank you for giving us a chance.'

Kim smiled. 'It's my pleasure.' She clapped her hands. 'So, this is how it's going to work. You'll start each day here, working with one keeper and one animal for the whole first week. You'll get the same training as all our other volunteers, which includes cleaning up after the animals. From tomorrow you'll need to be here ready at seven o'clock sharp. Okay?'

'Absolutely,' Sophia said.

'At the end of the week, you'll be tested on everything you've learned,' Kim added. 'So make sure you ask about anything that doesn't make sense.'

Ollie nodded. 'Can I ask something now?'

'Sure,' Kim said.

'Why poo? It's okay, of course,' he added quickly, catching Sophia's look. 'I'm just wondering.'

'It's a good question,' Kim said.

'People just flush their poop away. You absolutely wouldn't fish it out of the loo, check it out and find a use for it, would you?'

Ollie was shaking his head and starting to look ill.

Sophia tried not to laugh.

'But poo at the Zoo is super important. And knowing all about it is especially important for the animal you'll be taking care of.' Kim stood up. 'If you wait here,' she said. 'The keeper will be along in a moment to introduce you.'

Then she was gone.

Sophia's eyes drifted around the grid of animal habitats before her, wondering which one they'd be working in.

She could see Edna the echidna in the front habitat.

The spiny little cutie was marching around in the leaves looking for bugs.

'Poo!' Ollie said, his shoulders sagging a little again. 'It might be important, but, well – eww.' He followed Sophia's gaze. 'Edna would be good,' he said. 'Small poo.'

'And she's so sweet and gentle,' Sophia added.

'She's a monotreme,' Ollie said. 'That makes her special. Australia's one of only two places you can find them, and there's only five species of mammal that can lay eggs like her.'

'Yeah, but does that make her *poo* special?' Sophia asked.

'Good point.' Ollie had pulled out his notebook. He started spinning his pencil on his thumb, thinking.

Sophia wanted to learn to twirl a pen too, but she wasn't patient enough to practise. She looked around her. Behind Edna, two female red kangaroos were moving around looking very chilled. They looked a lot calmer than Sophia felt right now. Hidden off to the right, snug among the branches of eucalyptus, would be a koala or two. Beyond that, even more animals were starting their day. They could be working with any of them.

Sophia heard the crunching of boots on the dirt pathway. The owner of the footsteps was still out of sight. Sophia could barely resist the urge to jump up and find out who it was. Her whole body was tingling.

After an agonising few minutes, a figure strode into view. Dark hair framing a very familiar face . . .

Chapter 3

Meet Mateo

'Hey, kids. Ready to get to work?'

Sophia and Ollie sprung to their feet.

'We sure are,' Sophia said. She couldn't believe it. Standing before them was Sam, her favourite keeper.

Sophia had known Sam her whole life. She was like a cool aunt. Even Ollie was grinning now. If they were working with Sam, they knew which animal they'd be caring for – a koala.

'This way,' Sam said, heading back along the path. She stopped outside one of the koala habitats. Sophia saw two rakes, a dustpan and a bucket. Leaning against the fence were some cut branches. She knew in zoo talk, they were called 'browse'.

Ollie leaned forward. Sophia could tell he was trying to figure out which of the koalas they would be working with.

He knew them all by name, even when they were high up in the branches.

'I'm not sure if you've met him yet, but this is Mateo,' Sam said.

'Yes!' Ollie said. 'I was hoping it was him.'

Sam smiled. She led them around the outside of the habitat. Sophia heard Ollie suck in a little breath. Mateo was so close. Willow, Ella and the other koalas in Nura Diya Australia were usually high up in trees. Mateo was just above their head height, his face squished up against a branch.

They'd never been this close to a koala before.

Sophia looked down and saw little dark-green jellybean-shaped objects on the ground. Lots and lots of them.

She elbowed Ollie in the ribs and pointed. 'Eww. Is that what I think it is?'

'Yep!' Sam nodded.

'Now I have a question for you two,' she said.

Ollie brightened a little. He loved

animal facts so much he kept his own Fun Fact File in his notebook.

'How many poos do you think is a healthy number for a koala in twenty-four hours?'

Ollie chewed the inside of his cheek as he forced himself to look back into the habitat. Sophia followed his gaze.

'I'm going to say a hundred poos.'

Sophia spent a moment longer looking at the scattered jellybean shapes. 'I agree.'

'Pretty close,' Sam said. 'Between one hundred and two hundred "faecals", as we call them, is ideal in twenty-four hours. Some days it can get up to three hundred, though.'

'Three hundred!' Ollie's voice cracked. He swallowed. 'That's a lot of poo.'

'It sure is, and guess what? Your first job as volunteers is to count every single one.'

Ollie didn't even try to hide his horror. 'Count them?' he whispered. 'Like, one at a time?'

Sophia was feeling a little queasy now too. Cleaning was one thing, getting up close enough to count them was something else. Maybe Sam was kidding. 'Are you serious?' she asked.

'Yep. We do it every morning,' Sam replied. 'It's one of a koala keeper's most important jobs. It's the quickest and easiest way to keep track of Mateo's health.' She led them back to the gate and unlocked the latch.

Sophia covered her nose and mouth with her hand as she stepped into the habitat. Ollie pinched his nose.

They might have to count the poo, but they didn't have to smell it.

Sam started laughing. 'You can take your hands away. Trust me.'

Sophia felt the weight of the lanyard around her neck. She needed to do this. Her whole future at the Zoo depended on it. She let her hand drop to her side.

'Ollie,' she said, surprised. He shook his head. 'Ollie, it's okay.'

Reluctantly, he took a breath through his nose.

Despite being surrounded by more than a hundred koala poos, it wasn't stinky at all.

As Sam started sorting out fresh browse, Sophia moved closer to Ollie.

'How do you think we should count them?' she asked.

'I don't care,' Ollie said in a huff. 'I don't want to count something that's been in a koala's butt, even if it doesn't smell terrible.'

'Ollie, please,' Sophia said, quietly. 'This is important.'

He sighed. 'You're right. Sorry.' He looked thoughtfully at the ground around them. 'How about we take a section each and then add our counts together?'

'Great idea. I can start with that corner.' Sophia pointed to the area furthest from the gate.

Ollie agreed. 'I'll do this bit next to you and then we can do the other side.'

They both started to count, pointing at the dark-green pellets one at a time.

'One, two, three, four . . .' Sophia said under her breath.

'Eight, nine, ten . . .' Ollie's voice filtered into her brain.

'Eleven, twelve . . . ah, I mean five.' Sophia shook her head.

'What did you say?' Ollie asked. 'Oh,

crackers, I've lost count! Let's count in our heads.'

Sophia nodded. 'Good idea.'

It went much faster this time. Most of the poo was within bouncing distance of the branches that Mateo called home.

'Lucky koalas can't projectile poop,' Ollie said. 'If they could shoot their poo over a metre at high speed like penguins, it'd be everywhere!'

Sophia laughed. 'We'd be spending all our time running around trying to dodge poo bullets instead of cleaning up.'

By the time Ollie and Sophia had finished the first half of their count, Mateo was awake and watching them with sleepy eyes.

'Good morning, Mateo,' Ollie said. 'We're just, you know, counting your poop. Totally normal. Totally not weird.'

Sophia scrunched up her face. 'How strange would it be to have someone checking the toilet after you use it,' she said.

Mateo yawned, blinked and stretched.

Then he closed his eyes and resettled into a new position.

Ollie gave a little laugh. 'Mateo thinks it's no big deal at all.'

Chapter 4

What a mess!

'Well?' Sam asked.

Sophia and Ollie had been talking quietly, adding up their final numbers.

'Mateo's faecal count for today is one hundred and sixty-three,' Ollie said, a tiny tremor in his voice the only clue he was nervous about getting it right.

Sam smiled at them. 'That sounds good to me.'

Sophia and Ollie both grinned.

‘How can you be sure we got it right?’ Sophia asked.

‘I saw how you broke up the space to share the counting,’ Sam explained. ‘I do the same.’

She glanced at her watch. ‘I do need you guys to clean this poo up as quickly as you can now. We have some kids coming to meet Mateo in about an hour. Just rake it all up and put it in the bucket.’

Sophia nodded, trying not to let the disappointment show on her face. Ollie’s shoulders had slumped too. She took a deep breath and grabbed the rakes, handing one to Ollie.

‘I’ll start over there,’ he said, tiptoeing around the little pellets as he started to rake. The closer they got to Mateo, the harder it got to avoid the poo.

'Aah,' Ollie cried out, grabbing Sophia's arm as he lost balance.

She stumbled sideways and felt something slip under her foot.

'Oh, Ollie,' she groaned, lifting her boot. There was a bit of dark-green mush squashed on the edges of one sole. She gave a little shudder.

Ollie had fared much worse.

He had stumbled right into the pile of poo he'd been raking together.

'Seriously!' Ollie exclaimed. 'What a mess!'

Sophia and Sam did their best to hide their grins as Ollie scraped the poo off his boots, muttering.

Sophia glanced at Mateo. He was watching again and munching on a eucalyptus leaf. He looked like he might be grinning too.

'Sam, why doesn't the poo smell bad?' Sophia asked, as she scooped the last of the pellets into the bucket. 'Is it because Mateo only eats leaves?'

'It sure is,' Sam said, picking up a few pieces of poo. She held them out. Ollie and Sophia exchanged horrified looks.

Sam laughed. 'Go on,' she said. 'Take one.'

To Sophia's surprise, Ollie reached out and took one first. Maybe his encounter with the poo pile had helped. Sophia's brain was still screaming EWWW, but she took one too. It felt surprisingly un-poo-like.

'Smell it,' Sam said. She sniffed her poo pellet. 'Mmm,' she said. 'Lovely!'

Sophia and Ollie raised their hands slowly towards their faces.

Ollie brought the pellet closer and sniffed again. 'It smells like eucalyptus.'

'Eucalyptus leaves are so hard to digest that the poo comes out smelling just like the leaves,' Sam explained.

'Maybe we should make koala poo aroma bags for people to buy in the gift shop,' Ollie suggested.

Sam laughed. 'We've got an even better use for it,' she said. 'In fact,

Rohan's waiting for this bucket of poo at the back of the lion habitat.'

Sophia gasped. Sam had said the magic word – lion!

Ollie had never moved so fast. He picked up the bucket as Sophia ducked past and opened the gate. Sam followed with the rakes, shutting the gate behind them.

She paused as her radio crackled. 'Head out that way,' she said. 'I'll meet you at the giraffes.'

The path led them back onto one of the main walkways. Sophia had no idea why the lions needed koala poo, but she didn't care. They were actually going to work with the lions!

There were crowds now that the Zoo was open and there were lots of kids visiting for the school holidays. They stared and pointed as Sophia and Ollie carried their bucket of poo between them.

Sophia felt taller. She felt proud. Whatever her pass said, today she wasn't a visitor. She was working at the Zoo. They both were. She looked at Ollie and he grinned back.

At the bottom of the hill, they stopped. The African Savannah was spread out before them, with the glittering blue water of Sydney Harbour and the city stretched out behind.

They walked to the front, trying not to get in the way of all the people taking photos with the giraffes.

'Hey, Leggy,' Ollie said.

Leggy was what they had nicknamed their favourite giraffe. His real name was Jimiyu. He was walking towards some browse hanging near the fence.

He had just passed them when poo pellets came firing out of his bottom!

Sophia winced. 'So, the whole poo thing could be worse, I suppose. I guess penguins aren't the only projectile poopers.'

Ollie looked from the bucket to the mess in front of them. 'Yep. I'm good here.' They both laughed.

Leggy had finished eating and was just wandering off when they heard someone running up behind them. It was Sam.

'You're going to have to take the poo to Rohan by yourselves, sorry,' she said. Her forehead was creased, her usual smile gone.

'What's happened?' Ollie asked.

Sam pressed her lips together. 'We've had two rescued koalas brought into the Wildlife Hospital. A mum and joey. The mum is in bad shape. They'll need all the help they can get.'

Sophia felt her stomach tighten. It sounded bad.

The three of them headed past the chimpanzee community. Sophia loved watching their antics, but today she hurried by with barely a glance. All she could think about were those koalas.

Sam stopped where a path led up to the hospital. 'Once you've seen Rohan, head back to see Kim,' she said. 'There's no rush, but I'm sure she'll have something else you can help with. I'll see you tomorrow.'

Without waiting for a reply, she was gone.

Sophia spun towards Ollie.

'Soph,' he said, a warning in his voice. 'We have to do what Sam said. We can't go running after her to find out what's going on.'

'But the koalas –'

'Will be looked after,' he said. 'Plus, have you forgotten?' He gestured down another path. 'Lions!'

Sophia was torn, but she took a deep breath. Ollie was right. 'Okay,' she said. 'Let's go see Maya and Ato.'

Chapter 5

Poovlova

'Hey, you two,' Rohan said, as they walked up to the food preparation kitchen next to the lion habitat.

'Koala poo delivery as ordered,' Sophia said.

'Excellent! The perfect final ingredient for today's poovlova,' Rohan said as he took the bucket inside. 'Come on.'

Poovlova? Ollie mouthed silently to Sophia. Gross!

'They're not going to eat it, are they?' Sophia asked, not sure she wanted the answer.

Rohan laughed. 'No. Well, maybe . . . but unlikely.'

He placed their bucket beside four others. A quick glance told them they were all filled with poo.

'The poovlova is for Ato, Maya and the cubs,' Rohan explained. 'In the wild they'd come across lots of different smells and scents, so we give them poo to play with, as enrichment. Do you want to play a game of Whose Poos?'

Ollie stepped forward. He seemed to be coping a little better now. Sophia leaned in beside him. They scanned the row of buckets.

Sophia immediately recognised the poo in two of them. The other two, she wasn't sure. She looked at Ollie.

'I know that's kangaroo poo and they're elephant dung balls,' she said, pointing at two of the buckets.

'That's zebra,' Ollie said. 'They have grass sticking out, so they have to be a herbivore, plus they're a bit square-ish.' He pointed at the last bucket. 'And those are from the giraffes for sure,' he said. 'The dents give it away.'

'I don't get it,' Sophia said. 'Why are they dented?'

'Think about where their bottoms are,' Ollie said, raising his eyebrows.

Sophia couldn't stop the giggle that burst out. 'That poo had a long way to fall!'

'Plus they're small because they have four sections in their stomach, and they process food so well that there isn't much left to come out.'

Whose Poos?

'Right on all counts.' Rohan grinned at them. 'But you haven't had the full training experience until you've experienced this.' He was holding a bucket with a closed lid. He handed it to Ollie. 'Go on, open it.'

He did, and Sophia immediately wished he hadn't. She caught the barest glimpse of something black inside before she took three big steps backward.

Ollie had flung a hand up over his mouth and nose, holding the bucket out as far as he could.

'Oh, that's awful,' Sophia said.

Rohan took it with a laugh.

'You get used to it,' he said, lifting the lid completely to expose some gleaming black logs. 'These are lion poos. Lions are carnivores. They eat meat so their poo isn't very pleasant.'

'No kidding,' Ollie said, rubbing his nose.

'There are a few apples over there,' Rohan said, putting the lid back on the bucket. 'How about you two wash your hands, then head around to the side window and have something to eat while I make this poovlova for our lion friends?'

Sophia and Ollie washed their hands, then Sophia picked up two apples. She offered one to Ollie.

'Ew, how can you even think about food?'

Sophia shrugged, surprised at how hungry she was. In all the excitement, she hadn't noticed until now. She hadn't thought about the rescued koalas for a while either. She pushed her worry to the side. They were in the best hands.

Through the window of the habitat they saw Rohan waving at them to come closer.

They went right up to the glass and watched as Rohan tipped out piles of poovlova then headed back out through the gate.

A strange silence fell around them, then Ato and Maya prowled into the space. Immediately, Maya's amber eyes fixed on them. She was huge and amazing, and Sophia was glad to be behind the glass.

Maya's attention shifted as the five cubs bounded out. They were still small enough to be cute, but Sophia and Ollie knew they were already big enough to be dangerous.

One prowled over to the window.

Sophia could barely breathe.

The cub paused right in front of them, and lifted its paw to the glass.

'Hi, Khari,' Ollie whispered.

Sophia touched the glass on her side, staring into Khari's grey-blue eyes.

Then suddenly he was gone, pouncing on some grass off to the side.

Ollie let out a breath. 'That was . . . wow,' he whispered.

'Yeah,' Sophia said.

They watched another cub, Malika, approach a poovlova pile, circling and sniffing at the air. Suddenly, she plonked down, nuzzling and pushing the poo around.

'Is it possible for that to be awesome and yuck at the same time?' Ollie asked.

Sophia laughed. 'Totally!'

They watched the lions for a while as the crowds started to build around them, then they headed back. The Zoo was really busy now.

Everyone was watching the animals, except Sophia. She was keeping an eye out for the keepers and the volunteers.

She waved at some volunteers setting up a stand outside the southern corroboree frog habitat. When they waved back, Sophia straightened her shoulders, proud to be one of them.

'Hey, Earth to Soph?' Ollie said.

'Huh, sorry. What did you say?' Sophia asked. She'd barely registered that they'd made it back to the Taronga Institute of Science and Learning.

'I was asking where you think Kim might be,' he said.

Sophia didn't need to answer. Kim had just appeared at the top of the stairs.

'Fun morning?' she asked when they reached her.

Sophia nodded. 'So much fun. And it's not even lunchtime.'

'We're putting education kits together for some groups coming this week,' Kim said. 'It's not as much fun as poo, but would you like to help?'

'Absolutely,' Ollie said.

Sophia grinned at her best friend. She knew poo had been tough for him, but collecting facts was his specialty. It would be the perfect way to end their first day working in the Zoo.

Chapter 6

Mateo helps out

The early morning air was cool as Sophia and Ollie waited for Sam outside Mateo's habitat the next day.

They'd already cleaned the red-kangaroo habitat and Edna the echidna's home with a senior volunteer, Ben. He'd also shown them how to check all the gates, another important job they'd have to do. Sophia yawned.

She hadn't slept well. She'd been

worrying about the rescued koala and her joey. As she'd dozed and woken, and dozed and woken, she'd heard her dad watching television, waiting for her mum. After Sophia finally told him she couldn't sleep, he'd let Ruby, their old Aussie kelpie, sleep on her bed. But when Sophia eventually did sleep properly, she'd dreamed about poo.

Sophia had hoped to get an update from her mum, but she'd come in so late and left so early, she hadn't even seen her.

'Good morning,' Sam said. 'Before you ask, the koala joey is doing well.'

Sophia frowned.

'And what about the mum?' Ollie asked.

Sam sighed. 'It's touch and go. They had to operate, but she's stable for now. That's all I can tell you.'

Sophia and Ollie looked at each other and reluctantly let it drop.

'The exciting news is that today you'll be giving Mateo's poo a grade,' Sam said.

Sophia forced herself to focus. 'A grade?'

'Like a test at school?' Ollie asked.

Sam laughed. 'Not exactly. You use this card to work the score out.' Sam held out a piece of paper.

'A three is what you want,' she said. She opened Mateo's gate and they headed inside.

Sam looked at the ground and picked up two pellets, holding one in each hand. 'That's a perfect three,' she said, nodding to the one in her right hand. 'It's fully formed, not too hard, and a bit shiny with moisture.'

She offered it to Sophia.

'Gently squash it,' Sam said.

'Pardon?' Sophia asked, her stomach giving an uncomfortable flip.

Sam laughed. 'Give it a little squeeze. I know handling poo is weird, but you'll get used to it.'

Sophia had promised herself not to be grossed out by anything today. But squeezing a moist poo-pellet this early was almost too much.

'Okaaay,' Sophia said, swallowing. Her eyes narrowed as she noticed Ollie's shoulders shaking with silent laughter. She made a mental note to ensure the next poo squashing was his.

Sophia gently squeezed her fingers together. The poo only gave a little.

Sam squeezed the pellet in her hand. 'See how it crumbled,' she said. 'This one is more like a two. A few of these are okay, but we'd be worried if there was a lot. And of course, we don't want to see koala poo looking like soft-serve ice cream.'

‘I love soft serve,’ Ollie said, groaning. ‘Now I’ll never be able to eat it again.’

‘Don’t worry, Ollie,’ Sophia said. ‘There’s always vanilla ice cream – that looks nothing like poo.’

Sophia and Ollie got to work. Mateo was awake now and munching on some of the browse Sam was putting out.

‘They were pretty much all grade three in my sections,’ Sophia said as they finished raking the habitat and put all the poo in the bucket.

‘Definitely no soft serves here,’ Ollie agreed.

‘Today’s count was one hundred and ninety-three,’ Sophia told Sam. ‘I guess he ate a lot yesterday.’

‘Actually, his poo today matches what he was eating about a week ago,’ Sam explained. ‘It takes that long to digest.’

Mateo stretched and yawned.

'You should feel honoured,' Sam said. 'Mateo seems to like waking up when you're around. It's nice for you to be able to see him doing koala things, like eating, scratching –'

'And a lot of pooping!' Ollie exclaimed. He pointed at Mateo just as a jellybean-shaped pellet dropped to the ground.

'Thanks, Mateo. That makes today's count one hundred and ninety-four.' Ollie bent down and scooped the last poo into the bucket.

At the gate they heard Pixie's familiar laugh. They turned to see her waiting for them, pink hair peeking out the sides of her bucket hat.

Pixie wiggled her eyebrows. 'Do you two want to come and help out with some of biggest animals in the Zoo?'

'That has to be the elephants,' Ollie said. 'But their poop is enormous!'

'It is indeed.' Pixie laughed at the expression on his face. 'It's a crappy job, Ollie, but someone's gotta do it!' She grinned. 'Crappy. Get it?'

Ollie and Sophia just groaned and followed her out the gate.

Chapter 7

Backyard Team

'This is the staff-only pathway that leads to the Backyard Team area,' said Ollie.

'And the Wildlife Hospital,' said Sophia, quietly. 'Maybe we can check in on the koala mum and her joey.'

A giant open shed, bustling with activity, loomed to their right.

'Hi, Dad,' Ollie called out.

'About time you lot came to say hello,' he said. 'Working hard?'

'We sure are, Max,' Sophia said.

Ollie's dad had been in Taronga's Backyard Team for more than twenty years. He'd started the same week Sophia's mum had begun work at the hospital. Their families had been friends ever since.

Pixie waved as she walked towards him. 'Are you on elephant duty today, Max?'

'Yep. I'll just need to load up,' Max said. He was part way through tying a big blue barrel onto the back of a ute.

'Pixie, do you mind if we say a quick hi to Mum?' Sophia asked.

Pixie narrowed her eyes. 'This visit wouldn't have anything to do with getting an update on the two rescued koalas, would it?'

Sophia was already edging away,

dragging Ollie with her. 'Of course not.' She put on her most innocent expression, then gave up. 'Well, maybe just a little.'

Pixie folded her arms, but it was hard for her to stay serious for long. 'Be quick,' she said.

'Let's go, Ollie.' They sprinted towards the hospital doors.

As they arrived, one of the younger vet nurses, Lani, appeared around the side of the building, holding an armful of towels.

'Lani, do you know where my mum is?' Sophia asked.

'Sorry, Soph,' Lani said. 'She's with the koalas that were brought in yesterday. Sam just arrived to help.'

'We were with her when she got the call,' Ollie told her. 'How are they?'

Lani looked around, then leaned in

closer. 'We're actually a bit worried about the joey now.' Lani held up some soft towels. 'These are for her. I have to go. Sorry.'

'That's okay,' Sophia said. 'If anyone can make them better, it's Mum and Sam.' Sophia spoke with all the confidence she could muster and hoped with all her heart she was right.

Ollie and Sophia didn't talk as they walked back to Pixie and Max. They both knew how precious every koala life was, especially now they were endangered.

'Did you find anything out?' Pixie asked.

'They're worried about the joey . . .' Ollie's voice trailed off.

'Oh, dear.' Pixie was quiet a moment, then she smiled. 'Everyone in that wildlife hospital is incredible. You know that. Everything will work out.'

Sophia glanced at Ollie. He was nodding in agreement, so she forced herself to nod too.

Ollie hopped into the seat next to his dad and Sophia got into a buggy with Pixie driving. The buggy bounced out of the shed. Even with no doors or windows, the electric engine was very quiet.

The first part of the drive took them around the back of the lions and past the Roar and Snore tents.

Sophia saw Ollie pointing out the window of the ute in front.

She sat up straighter. Through the bamboo trees she could see the back of a habitat, and the distinctive orange and black stripes of the Sumatran tigers.

Sophia knew that Ollie would be asking his dad if he'd seen the cubs that day.

They were intense-looking big cats and would be fearsome hunters in the wild, but Ollie still talked about them like they were fluffy little kittens.

She looked around as they drove past the Free Flight Birds ampitheatre area. She tried to enjoy the ride, but she couldn't get thoughts of the rescued koalas out of her head. In fact, she barely noticed when Max turned onto one of the Zoo's main pathways and stopped in front of them.

'I'll just check the load before we drive through this crowd,' he called out, hopping down to tighten the straps.

Pixie cut the engine and spun in her seat, startling Sophia. 'Enough of the frowny face,' she said. 'How about another poop joke?'

Ollie's dad laughed. 'No, thanks, Pixie,' he said. 'They stink!'

Ollie stuck his head out the window. 'Yeah, Pixie,' he said. 'Poop jokes aren't my favourite . . . but they're a solid number two.'

Max chuckled as Pixie roared with laughter. Ollie was laughing too. Sophia let herself smile. The jokes were terrible, but her spirits started to lift.

Max rolled forward, flicking the switch that turned on a loud rhythmic beeping sound. It was effective. The crowds parted as they drove slowly towards the centre of the Zoo.

Groups of visitors turned from the animals to stare at them. And so did Mary the sun bear.

The elephant keepers Chen and Ryan were there to meet them at the back gate.

'Max, you're with me,' Ryan said. 'We need to get those barrels in place.'

'And you lot are coming with me,' Chen said, grinning.

There was a stack of large shovels lined up against a fence.

Ollie jumped to the ground. 'Let's do this!'

Chapter 8

Elephant experiment

Sophia looked at Ollie in surprise. He'd come a long way from worrying about a bit of koala poo on his shoe. In fact, his body was jiggling with so much excitement, he was almost bouncing.

Chen unlocked the gate, grabbed three shovels and waved them all through.

'I can't believe it, Soph,' Ollie said. He was talking fast. 'We're going inside. We're actually going inside the elephant habitat. For real.'

'I don't want to poop on your party, but the Asian elephants aren't in here with us,' Pixie said from behind them. 'They're up in the top paddock.'

'I know,' Ollie said, glancing over his shoulder. 'But it's still SO cool. We've never been allowed in here before.'

He'd come to a stop behind Chen, and was turning slowly, taking it all in. Distracted by Ollie's excitement, Sophia didn't notice the soft obstacle on the ground until a millisecond too late.

Her arms cartwheeled as her foot slipped out from under her.

She grabbed the only thing in reach – Ollie. Gripping his arm, Sophia tried to pull herself upright, but Ollie wasn't stable either. Sophia's momentum sent them both tumbling . . .

. . . right into a giant squishy pile of poo.

Everyone stood frozen in stunned silence.

'Well, Soph,' Ollie said, his voice surprisingly calm. 'Thanks to that experiment, I can now confirm that elephant poo . . . doesn't stink.'

Something between a snort and a laugh burst from Sophia. Who was this person and what had he done with Ollie?

'Yes,' she said. 'I believe your conclusion is correct.'

'In fact,' Ollie gave the air a little sniff, 'based on my current sample, I'd say these elephants have been eating a fair bit of hay.'

As everyone started laughing, Sophia finally dared to look at Ollie.

She scrunched up her nose. 'Sorry,' she mouthed silently.

'You owe me something really big,' Ollie said. 'In fact . . .' He pointed at the giant pile of poo he was sitting in. 'You owe me something huge.'

'That's fair.' She knew she'd be paying for this for a while.

Everyone was still laughing as they helped Sophia and Ollie to their feet.

'Graceful,' Pixie said, wiping tears from her cheeks.

They cleaned up as best they could. It was like being covered in mud and when it dried, it kind of flaked off.

'There's about a hundred kilos of poo a day per elephant,' Pixie said. 'We've got a fair chunk of today's quota to get cleaned up and ready for processing.' She pointed to a wheelbarrow sitting empty nearby. 'We better get moving.'

'My dad weighs almost a hundred kilos,' Ollie said.

Sophia laughed. 'I just pictured your dad made from elephant poo. You know, like the mud men we used to make, with hairy grass bits sticking out and –'

'Okay, I get it,' Ollie interrupted. 'Now you owe me for that mental picture too.'

The poo was heavy, and there was plenty of it, but the four of them got the job done quickly.

'Last one,' Ollie said, upending his shovel into the wheelbarrow.

Sophia and Ollie wandered over to where Pixie was standing looking at a small container with Chen. They both had latex gloves on.

'Look,' Pixie said. Sophia and Ollie took a small step back as she thrust a particularly moist, large elephant dung ball towards them. 'You can still see all the grass and leaves from the branches they've eaten.' She pulled the poo apart, like she was breaking open a bread roll. 'What they eat goes through them so quickly, only about half of it gets digested. You'll like this, Ollie,' she said, stepping towards him. 'There's so much fibre in their poo that you can even make paper out of it!'

Ollie leant forward to look. 'That's actually really cool.'

Max wandered towards them. 'Is my poo delivery ready?' he asked.

'Yep, all ready for processing,' Chen told him.

'Great.' He looked at Pixie, Sophia and Ollie. 'I'm dropping this load but also picking up some compost for the gardens, so I'll be a while. Pixie, are you okay to take Ollie and Soph back with you?'

'No problem,' Pixie said. 'But first, I think these two have earned a Food Market treat.'

The Taronga Food Market was bustling with hungry holiday visitors, but after washing their hands, Sophia and Ollie found a quiet table outside. It had a perfect view of the two elephants at the Zoo.

Their names were Tang Mo and Pak Boon, but Sophia and Ollie called them by their nicknames, Mo and Boony, like the keepers did.

'Look,' Sophia said with a laugh. Pak Boon had plonked herself in a pool of water and was swooshing her trunk around, then spraying it in the air.

A little group of kids by the fence were squealing with delight.

Pak Boon was thirty years old and Tang Mo was only twenty-four, so they were both young elephants.

Tang Mo reached up her trunk, delicately plucking a thin branch from a feeder hanging above her head.

'Elephants have over forty-thousand muscles in their trunks,' Ollie said. 'They can knock down a tree or pick up a blade of grass.'

'I hope you've added that fun fact to your file,' Pixie said, plonking a tray with juice bottles and two heaped plates of hot chips on the table in front of them. 'It'll come in handy for keeper talks. I've started carrying a little notebook now too.'

Sophia sucked in a breath. 'I didn't know volunteers did talks,' she said, trying to keep her voice steady.

She wasn't shy, but the idea of standing up in front of a group of strangers still made her stomach twist up in knots.

'Guests ask us questions sometimes.' Pixie dipped a chip in some sauce and popped it in her mouth. 'But you definitely give talks as keepers.'

'Oh, yeah.' Sophia picked up a chip too. She'd forgotten that.

A kookaburra squawked somewhere close by. Ollie and Sophia looked up into a nearby tree where a big kookaburra was watching them hopefully.

Ollie pointed his finger sternly at the bird. 'Dream on,' he said, grabbing a handful of chips and stuffing them in his mouth. 'Go and find a lizard or a mouse for lunch.'

'We're not feeding you,' said Sophia. 'No way!'

The kookaburra laughed before taking off and flying low past their table.

'I guess we know which animal is the best hunter,' Pixie said. 'Let's put these things in the bin so we don't encourage him.'

Chapter 9
Poo-shake

Sophia couldn't stand still as they waited for Sam to start day three of their training. She couldn't decide if she was more excited about the day ahead or more worried that she would hear bad news about the koala mum and her joey.

Over dinner the night before, her mum had told her that they were stable, but she'd still had her worry-smile on.

Sophia put her elbows on the railing

beside Ollie. 'Sorry I'm so fidgety, Ollie.' She let out a big breath.

Ollie didn't seem to have noticed. He was looking seriously at the habitat.

'I think Mateo's poo count is down today,' he said. 'Remember how Sam told us she counted one section of the ground then figured out the total.'

'Yeah,' Sophia said.

'Well, I just did that,' he explained. 'And it's less than a hundred.'

'You'd fit right in with our wildlife pathologists.' They both spun around. Sam was behind them, looking impressed.

Sophia saw Ollie straighten his shoulders. She knew being a wildlife scientist would be his dream come true.

They got to work, counting and raking. Ollie had been right. Mateo's poo count was only ninety-four.

'I'm not too worried about one day,' Sam explained, as the three of them peered into the bucket.

'If it takes about a week from eating to pooping the food out,' Ollie said, 'then he probably didn't eat much last week.'

Sophia and Ollie looked over at the browse Sam was clearing up. 'There are so many leaves left,' Sophia said. 'Does that mean he's not eating properly today either?'

'No, they only eat the fresh tippy stuff.' Sam pulled down a branch, pointing at some paler, small shoots. 'He missed this bit, so we'll save that for him. But on the whole, I'd say today is pretty good. Koalas are very picky.'

Sam started organising the new browse as she spoke.

‘There are over seven hundred species of eucalyptus trees in Australia. Koalas can only eat about fifty to seventy of them and, out of that, a koala will only choose to eat ten to twelve species.’

Sophia watched Mateo stretch and settle in the fork of a branch. ‘Like how I eat baby spinach but not rocket leaves?’ she asked.

Sam nodded. ‘But koalas won’t eat anything except their favourite leaves, even if they’re starving.’

‘I get that, Mateo,’ Ollie said, looking up at him. ‘I feel kind of the same about broccoli.’ He shuddered. ‘They’re all . . . well, tree-ish.’

‘So, what now?’ Sophia asked, daring to hope it might be a visit to the hospital. She crossed her fingers behind her back.

Sam looked at them thoughtfully. 'Well, I do need to go to the hospital to give the rescued joey some food. Follow me and bring the poo.'

Sophia barely held in a squeal.

'Sam,' she said, half skipping to keep up with her as they headed down the hill. 'I've been thinking. If grown-up koalas are so picky, how do you know the joey will eat what you give her?'

'She's still a bit young for leaves,' Sam said. 'But it's vital we get her gut ready to eat them, and her mum can't help with that right now. So you're going to be the mum and make her a poo-shake.'

Ollie let out a strangled noise, and Sophia felt the blood drain from her face.

She'd counted poop, sniffed it, squished it and even sat in it, but this was a whole other level.

This is all part of the test, she said to herself. The test to see if we're ready to be volunteers. Pull it together, Sophia!

'A poo-shake?' she squeaked.

'Please tell me it doesn't actually look like a milkshake?' Ollie said. 'Because you've already ruined soft serve for me . . . and pavlova.' He didn't just look pale. He looked green.

'No, not a milkshake,' Sam said.

Ollie exhaled. 'Thank goodness.'

'It's more like a little joey-sized thickshake,' Sam finished with a grin.

Chapter 10
Feeding time

Sam led Sophia and Ollie to a room in the Wildlife Hospital with some lab equipment and a computer.

'We can enter Mateo's details here,' she said. 'Who wants to give it a go?'

'Can I?' asked Ollie.

'Sure,' Sam said, sliding a stool around behind him.

Sophia watched closely as Sam talked Ollie through the different screens to enter the poo count and a browse score to record how well Mateo ate.

Sophia took a deep breath. She loved spending time out in the animal habitats, but being in the hospital was what had her the most excited.

'I can't believe I'm about to say this, but can we make the poo thickshake now?'

Sam laughed and nodded, then led them through another set of doors. Lani was standing at a bench, a couple of containers in front of her.

'Hey, Lani,' Sam said. 'Where are we up to?'

Lani screwed up her nose. 'The poo has been soaking for an hour. I can't say this is my favourite part of the job.'

Sam laughed. 'Fair enough.'

'Why is it soaking?' Ollie asked.

‘When a joey is shifting from milk to solid food,’ Sam explained, ‘the mum produces something called “pap”. It’s full of all the micro bacteria they need to get their gut ready for eucalyptus leaves.’

‘Is it like mushed-up leaves or something?’ Ollie asked.

‘Kind of,’ Lani said. ‘It’s just been through a certain amount of koala processing first.’

Sophia glanced at Ollie.

‘I’ve got a bad feeling about this,’ he muttered.

Lani laughed. ‘The joey massages its mum’s bottom to get the special sort of poo – it’s not poo at all really . . .’

Ollie groaned. His face had gone very pale again. ‘That’s enough info. I get it.’

‘But there’s more,’ Lani said. ‘What

the joey wants isn't the normal grade three poos. She needs the stuff that comes after it.'

'Because our mum koala is sick, we're going to need to give the baby a helping hand,' Sam said.

Ollie took a small step backwards. 'Can I just take notes?'

Sam and Lani burst into laughter.

'Don't worry, you're not going to have to massage any koala bottoms!' Sam said.

Sophia had never felt more relieved. 'Come on, Ollie.' She gave him a gentle nudge with her elbow. 'You've made me plenty of thickshakes at home.'

'Not helpful, Soph,' he said.

He crossed his arms, but eventually shrugged, a small smile creeping across his face.

'I guess I won't be able to have thickshakes *or* soft serve from now on,' he said. 'So, how do we make this delightful drink?'

Lani held up a small container.

'It's pretty simple,' Sam said. 'We've already soaked the pellets to get the mucous coating on them to swell. The next step is to gently stir the mixture to loosen the mucous sacs. Ollie, I'll get you to do that, and then syringe off the mucous so we can mix it with water.'

'Lucky me,' Ollie said.

Even though he sounded grossed out, Ollie took his job very seriously. Sam and Lani were so impressed they even let him filter the mix to remove any larger particles and collect the liquid.

He held up the container proudly.

'That's one delicious drink for our joey,' Sam said.

The door clicked open behind them, and Sophia's mum, Donna, stepped through.

'Mum, Ollie made the joey a poo-shake,' Sophia said, racing over to give her a hug.

'Brilliant. Well done, Ollie! That's

actually why I'm here.'

Lani took over, scooping the mixture into a different tub and grabbing a large clear syringe.

'This way,' Donna said, leading them out through a second door and down a narrow corridor.

Sophia's heart was racing. Were they really going to be allowed to be there when her mum fed the joey?

While some of the rooms they passed were empty, there was lots of activity in one, so they stopped to look through the viewing window.

The room was filled with people in turquoise scrubs. As one of the vet nurses moved back from a table, Sophia sucked in a little breath.

'Is that a gorilla?' she asked, her eyes wide.

'She's getting some dental work,' Sam explained.

It was amazing to see how big the gorilla was.

She was unconscious, and her mouth was wide open, just like a person at the dentist.

‘It’s a huge thing to get one of our gorillas in here. It takes lots of planning. You’re lucky to see it, but our little joey will be getting hungry so we’d better go.’

‘Come on, Soph,’ Ollie said.

Torn between wanting to watch and seeing the joey, Sophia followed Sam into another room.

A vet nurse was cradling a bundle of towels. Sophia spotted a little grey ear poking out.

The towels flopped open as he handed the joey over to Donna. It was tiny and looked exactly like the koala toys in the gift shop.

‘She’s so small and cute,’ Ollie said.

‘Ollie and Soph, meet Billie,’ Donna said. ‘We called his mum Blinky, so she became Bill, or Billie.’

‘Like the books!’ Ollie said.

Donna nodded. ‘Without her mum around for now, we’re going to have to get her eating. Her life depends on it.’

Sophia looked at Ollie. He gave her a gentle push. ‘Go on, Soph,’ he whispered. ‘Ask her.’

‘Do you think . . . Could I possibly?’ Sophia wanted to feed the joey so badly that she ran out of words.

Donna nodded and smiled.

Sophia could feel her heart beating so loudly she thought Ollie could probably hear it too.

Sam filled the syringe with the mixture and handed it to Sophia.

Holding her breath, Sophia put the syringe to the corner of Billie’s mouth. ‘Here we go,’ she said.

Nothing happened for a moment, then she saw the joey's mouth move.

Donna smiled. 'She's taking it.'

Sophia let out her breath and grinned at Ollie. They'd made that happen. The joey was eating! She just hoped it would be enough.

Chapter 11
The test

Sophia's heart was full to bursting as she worked beside Ollie, finishing their jobs in Mateo's habitat. She couldn't believe it was already day four.

The sun was shining, and she was living her zookeeping dream. Sam had been watching and taking notes.

As Sophia started packing up under Mateo's sleepy gaze, she thought about the koala joey. On the drive home the afternoon before, her mum had told her Billie was doing much better. Their poo-shake had done the trick.

'What's your poo count today?' Sam asked, as she followed them out and closed the gate.

'Back to normal. One hundred and seventy-eight poos,' Ollie said.

Sam smiled. 'And a good range for faecal count is . . . ?'

'Between one hundred and two hundred,' Ollie confirmed.

'Correct,' Sam said. She made a note on her clipboard. 'Sophia, what else do we check?'

'Today's poo was a grade three,' she said. 'And the browse was a healthy one.'

Sophia knew they weren't just passing the test. They were acing it.

Sam was beaming at them. 'Now

I need you two to go and help Ben finish cleaning the other animal habitats. We have a group of kids who have come all the way from Dalgety for a special zoo experience, including a koala talk.'

'Can we watch?' Ollie asked.

'Of course.' Sam latched the gate behind them. 'You can help if you like. Who knows, maybe you'll be doing keeper talks one day.'

Sophia's confidence evaporated as butterflies exploded in her stomach.

Ollie was nodding and grinning. Sophia knew he'd be brilliant at talking to groups. He could keep so many cool bits of information in his head and pull them out on demand. But public speaking was the last thing Sophia wanted to do. When she stood in front of strangers, it was like everything she knew got sucked from her brain.

She forced herself to breathe and keep smiling. They weren't even official volunteers. Not yet. It wasn't like *she* had to do the talk.

Sophia's keeper-talk worries quickly faded as they helped Ben tidy up Edna the echidna's home. Then they shifted to the kangaroo yard.

'Why do I feel like I'm being followed?' Ollie said, as he dragged a rake across the dirt.

'Because you are,' Sophia said with a laugh, leaning on her rake.

He turned to find the smaller of the two female kangaroos behind him. Ben handed Ollie some browse for the kangaroo to nibble on.

'Hungry?' Ollie asked.

The kangaroo moved closer.

'I think she likes me,' Ollie said, a huge grin on his face.

When they were done, Ben led them out and shut the gate. 'Thanks, guys – you're awesome.'

'Happy to help,' Sophia said.

She followed Ollie back to the bench seats and sat down.

Ollie's stomach growled. 'I really need some food too. Do we have time?' he asked.

'I hope so,' Sophia said. She checked her watch. 'We have to meet Sam at ten-thirty. Let's be quick.'

Picking up their bags, they headed inside to the common area on the top floor. Sitting among all the volunteers and Zoo staff, Sophia felt happier than she'd ever been.

Lots of people were waving to them and saying hello, just like they belonged.

'Soph,' Ollie said. There was an edge

to his voice that made her heart start racing. He nodded over her shoulder.

Sophia spun in her chair. The door to the Keepers Kitchen was all glass. There were a few people in the room, but her attention was on Sam – she was already there, gesturing urgently as she talked.

One of the keepers was shaking his head, while another lady had put both hands over her mouth. Then Sam left the room, walking quickly down the stairs and out of the building.

'That looked intense,' Ollie said.

'Do you think it might be . . .' Sophia's voice trailed off.

'Billie?' Ollie finished. 'I hope not.'

Then Sophia had a terrible thought. Billie wasn't the only koala being cared for in the hospital . . .

'What if something else has happened

to Billie's mum, Blinky? Let's go and ask Ben. He might know.'

Sophia knocked on the glass door and Ben let them inside.

'What's happening?' Sophia asked. 'Where did everyone go?'

'Not sure,' he said. 'But Sam said to help you get Mateo's scores in while we wait for her to get back.'

Sophia squeezed her lips together. She wasn't sure she believed him, but she sat at the computer. Ben logged her in, then got on with other jobs while she entered Mateo's poo and food details. When she finished, she glanced at her watch.

'Ollie,' she whispered, pointing at her wrist. It was ten-forty. 'Where's Sam?'

Through the door, Sophia saw a Taronga cap bobbing up the stairs. But it wasn't Sam, it was Kim.

She swiped her pass and came into the room. Her forehead was creased with worry.

'We've got a problem,' she said.

Chapter 12
Plan B

'What's going on?' Ben asked.

Kim took a deep breath. 'Well, we have twenty-five kids about to arrive for their eleven o'clock koala-keeper talk and no guarantee Sam will be back.'

'What's happened?' Ollie asked.

Kim looked at them, her face serious. 'It's Blinky.'

Sophia sucked in a breath. 'Is she okay?'

Kim gave her head a little shake. 'I'm afraid not,' she said. 'But your mum and the Wildlife Hospital team are doing everything they can.'

Sophia felt her chest tighten.

'I need a Plan B,' Kim said. 'I can't just cancel.'

'You could get Ollie and Sophia to do the talk,' Ben suggested. 'They know their stuff. Sam was joking this morning that they might put her out of a job.' He shrugged. 'Just a thought.'

'Actually, that's not a bad plan,' Kim said. 'You two could be on standby with me in case Sam doesn't make it.'

'Really?' Ollie said, his eyes shining.

'Really,' she said.

Sophia forced herself to keep breathing.

Kim flew into action. 'Okay, let's

head up there now. You two can have a think about the different things you could talk about.'

'*If* Sam doesn't make it,' Sophia said quietly. 'Right?'

'Yes, of course,' Kim said. 'I'm sure she will, but it doesn't hurt to be prepared.'

Ollie didn't stop talking as Kim swiped them through the door and out the back to the habitats. But Sophia barely heard a word through the roaring in her ears. What if they *did* have to do the talk? What if she forgot everything she was supposed to say? What if she made a fool of herself in front of all those kids?

'Soph,' Ollie said. It was clear it wasn't the first time he'd said her name. 'It's okay to be nervous,' he said. 'I'm nervous too.'

Sophia looked at him. 'Really?'

'Yeah,' he said. 'What if I totally blank?'

Sophia's eyes opened wide. 'That's what I was thinking,' she said. 'I thought you were totally cool with it.'

'Cool?' he said. 'Nah, I feel a bit like I'm going to throw up. But we'll be together. We can help each other. Right?'

Sophia filled her lungs and let out a slow breath.

'Yeah,' she said.

'We've got this,' Ollie said quietly.

'We do,' Sophia said. 'Together.'

'Together,' Ollie repeated.

They could hear a babble of voices. The kids had arrived. Sophia glanced at her watch. Five minutes to go. She looked along the path. There was no sign of Sam. Kim's radio crackled.

'*Sam to Kim, over.*'

Sophia glanced at Ollie.

'Kim here, over.'

'*I'm not going to make it,*' Sam said. '*Sorry.*'

'All good. We'll go to plan B,' Kim said.

Sophia swallowed and she was sure everyone could hear her racing heart.

'Well, kids. You're up,' Kim said. 'Ben will stay with you. I'll go get our special guests.' She smiled. 'Good luck.'

Excited voices got louder as the kids appeared on the path. Kim organised the group around the railing where they could all see Ollie, Sophia and Mateo in the habitat.

'We have an extra special treat for you today,' Kim said. 'You're getting a keeper talk from two of our volunteers-in-training. I'd like to introduce Sophia and Ollie.'

The kids clapped wildly.

Mateo opened his eyes and stretched. He didn't look worried. Had he just given Sophia a reassuring wink?

'Hi, everyone,' Ollie said. 'This is Mateo. He's nearly five years old and weighs about ten kilograms. But let's get straight to the fun facts. Who can guess how many poos he'll do in a day?'

The kids all laughed.

Sophia couldn't help smiling as twenty-five hands shot up in the air. She pointed at a little girl with freckles.

'A hundred?' she guessed.

'Close,' Sophia said. Her voice was a bit wobbly, but no one seemed to notice. 'Can you believe when Mateo is healthy, he'll poo between a hundred and two hundred times every day?'

A little boy's hand shot up. Ollie nodded his way. 'Does he poo when he's asleep?'

'Not usually,' Ollie said. 'He can, but he does most of his pooping while he's awake, and that's only for about three to four hours a day.'

The boy giggled. 'That's not a lot of time for a super lot of pooping.'

'Very true,' Ollie said.

They told the kids all about counting and grading the poo. There were lots of groans when Ollie shared his soft-serve story and told them how koala joeys get the pap from their mum.

There were plenty of *ewwws* when Sophia bent down and picked up a fresh poo. They got even louder when she lifted the poo to her nose.

'Mmmm,' Sophia said. She looked around the group, grinning. 'Who wants a sniff?'

Most of the kids shook their heads, but the little girl with freckles slowly raised her hand.

'Is it bad?' she asked.

'Have a smell, and you can tell me.'

The girl took a sniff and her eyes opened wide. 'It's like the stuff Mum makes me smell when I have a cold.'

'That's eucalyptus,' Sophia said, 'from gum leaves.'

Sophia was enjoying herself so much, it was only when the group was giving them a huge clap at the end that she realised four more people had appeared quietly at the back.

She had no idea how long they'd been there, but smiling over the heads of the kids were Sam, Pixie, Ollie's dad and her mum.

Chapter 13

Bird magic

They'd done it. A real koala-keeper talk, with a real audience. Sophia could hardly believe it.

'You kids were fabulous,' Kim said. 'Good information but funny too.'

Sophia felt heat in her cheeks.

'Thank you,' Ollie said, his cheeks bright red. 'It was scary, but once we got going it was okay.'

'You guys were AWESOME!' Pixie

said, grabbing them both in big bear hugs. 'That was one of the best keeper talks I've heard.'

Sam had been helping in the habitat, but now she headed over to Sophia and Ollie. 'I saw the last part and it was terrific. I knew you could do it,' she said.

'If you're all here, does that mean Blinky is going to be okay?' Sophia asked, looking hopefully from Sam to her mum.

'I think so,' her mum said. 'We had a bit of a scare. She needed emergency surgery, but she's stable again now. I'm hoping we'll be able to reunite her with Billie when she's recovered.'

Ollie let out a big breath. 'That's awesome news.'

'I bet you two could use some food,'

Pixie said. 'Who's up for a Food Market lunch?'

Right on cue, Ollie's stomach growled. 'Yes, please,' he said, grinning. 'I can't believe it's only lunchtime. I'm pooped!'

Everyone was laughing as they headed down the hill.

Ollie and Sophia were still buzzing on the last morning of their training.

Sophia almost wished the school holidays were over so she could tell all their friends at school about the keeper talk. She couldn't wait to hear them laugh about the bits where they almost forgot what to say and the funny questions from the kids.

'You certainly inspired yesterday's visitors,' Sam said as they lifted the old browse over the fence. 'Kim sent me an email from the group organiser saying half the kids now want to be kid zookeepers, just like you. But your work isn't done yet.' She stood up straight and handed Ollie the bucket. 'Could you take the poo over to the dingoes for me? You can drop this browse to the Australian Rainforest Aviary on the way too, please. Then you're done!'

'No problem,' Sophia said. She stepped out through the gate and bundled the browse up in her arms. It was scratchy and she could barely see over the top, but she didn't care. 'Ready, Ollie?'

'Right behind you,' he said.

Sophia felt light and happy as they

wound through the holiday crowds along the path to the aviary. She handed the browse over to one of the bird keepers, knowing it would soon be creating lots of enrichment for all the Zoo's special Australian bird species.

Then she took a turn carrying the poo bucket for the second half of the walk to wuragal nura, Dingo Country.

Just like with the lions, koala poo was in high demand for Taronga's two dingoes, Kep Kep and Warada.

Sophia and Ollie were more surprised to discover the dingoes' other favourite enrichment ingredient – Vegemite.

'You don't get much more Australian than that,' Sophia said.

'Don't tell anyone, but I'm glad we didn't do our training here,' Ollie said quietly.

'I agree,' Sophia said. 'I know they're not technically dogs, but I clean up enough of Ruby's stinky dog poo at home already.'

Ollie scrunched up his face. 'We better hurry. We said we'd meet Pixie at twelve.'

They raced down the hill from Nura Diya Australia.

'See you later, Mackenzie,' Ollie called out as they dashed past the cassowary.

Sophia pulled up short as they ran past the capybaras. Ollie narrowly avoided crashing straight into her back.

'Did you see that?' Sophia said, pointing. 'Look, it's doing it again. That capybara is eating poop.'

'Aww, guys,' Ollie said, putting his face in his hands. 'That's really not cool.'

'I'm sure there's a good explanation,' Sophia said, as they started to jog away.

'Probably,' Ollie said, shaking his head.

Pixie was waiting by the top elephant paddock, watching Pak Boon playing in the water. 'Let's go see the Free Flight Birds,' she said. 'My friend Alison is presenting the show today. She started off as a volunteer too.'

They headed past Mary the sun bear and Esmeralda and Lance, the old Aldabra giant tortoises. They were enjoying the midday sun beside the pond.

The Free Flight Birds seating was packed, but Sophia, Ollie and Pixie found some room to one side.

'Pixie,' Ollie asked, quietly. 'Why do capybaras eat their poo?'

'Are you sure you want to know?' she asked.

Ollie nodded, but his expression was a little unsure.

'They mostly eat aquatic plants and

microbes, which are hard to digest. Their poo has lots of good protein and stuff from what they ate the day before, so they eat it again. It means they get to digest the food twice.'

Ollie shook his head. 'I wish I hadn't asked.'

'No, you don't.' Sophia nudged him with her elbow.

'You're right,' he agreed. 'It's gross, but kind of clever.'

A hush fell as the sound of birdsong filled the air. With a *whoosh* the birds arrived, swooping low over their heads. Sophia's breath caught in her throat. It was always magical to see them fly so close.

They'd been watching for a while when Alison appeared beside them. 'You must be Ollie,' she said quietly. 'I need you to stand up here.' She pointed at a spot beside her. 'Sophia, you head over to that side near the front. Arnold will meet you there.'

Sophia's heart was hammering in her chest as she did as she was told. She'd seen this show enough times to know why they got people to stand up. She'd never been chosen before. Pixie was grinning, not surprised at all.

Sophia reached Arnold just as Alison's voice filtered across the space.

'Ollie is going to hold his arm out very still,' she said. Sophia looked up to see a gorgeous black bird land on Ollie's hand. 'Monotoca here is a female red-tailed black cockatoo,' Alison told the crowd. 'But unlike the males that are black with red tails, she has gorgeous yellow speckles and yellow-orange stripes on hers.'

Even from the distance, Sophia could see Ollie beaming.

'Hold out your hand, Soph,' Arnold said.

She heard the *ahhhh* from the crowd a moment before Monotoca glided low across their heads, landing on Sophia's hand. She was surprisingly heavy.

Sophia knew Arnold was talking to the crowd, but she didn't hear a word. There was only her and this beautiful bird.

She blinked as Monotoca flew off again, then everyone was cheering as Alison thanked Sophia and Ollie for their help.

Sophia was still struggling to speak as the crowds filed out after the show.

'That. Was. MAGIC,' Ollie said.

'I thought you deserved a treat,' Pixie said. 'So I called in some favours.'

Sophia gave her a big hug. 'Thank you so much.'

Suddenly, Pixie's radio crackled. She stepped away to answer it. She was back a moment later, clipping it back on her belt.

'No time to explain,' Pixie said. 'Kim radioed me. They need you back there, right now.'

Chapter 14

The surprise

Ollie shot a glance at Sophia as Pixie led them up the stairs and into the common area. The room was packed. There was Sophia's mum and Ollie's dad, along with almost everyone they'd worked with that week or knew at the Zoo. Sam was standing with Kim to one side. She waved them over.

Sophia's stomach twisted into knots. Had they done something wrong?

She glanced at Ollie. His forehead was furrowed.

'Thanks for coming, everyone,' Kim said. 'As you all know, Sophia and Ollie have been training with Sam this week. It was to be their first week of training, with a second week to follow. Things have changed.'

Sophia felt sick and she saw all the blood drain out of Ollie's face. He swallowed. What had happened?

'Sam, would you like to explain?' Kim said.

'Of course,' she said. 'Sophia and Ollie might be younger than even our youngest YATZ participants, but they have demonstrated everything we expect from our volunteers and more.'

Sam smiled, and Sophia felt her whole body relax.

'When I was called away to help Blinky, our injured koala, these two kids stepped up and gave some young visitors a keeper talk they'll never forget.'

Ollie looked stunned.

'You were right, Ollie,' Sophia whispered to him. 'We did it . . .'

'. . . together,' he said, and gave her a big hug.

'We're not going to wait for a second week of training,' Kim said. She turned to face Sophia and Ollie. She was holding two Taronga volunteer shirts. 'I'm proud to confirm you are Taronga Zoo's youngest-ever official volunteers.'

The room erupted in cheers, clapping and whistles. Sophia held the shirt close. She could hardly believe it. Judging by the stunned expression on Ollie's face, he was feeling the same.

'This doesn't mean your training is over,' Kim said, when the room had settled. 'We never stop learning, but you've more than earned the right to wear these shirts.'

As everyone headed back to work, Kim showed Sophia and Ollie where they would go to sign in for passes on the days they were at the Zoo.

Sophia even got to swipe them through to the animal habitats.

'On Monday, you'll be coming back here,' Kim said. She walked them to the habitat right in front of them. 'Your next week of training will be a little more prickly. You'll be learning about all the work we're doing with echidnas and the secrets our scientist are finding out about their quills.'

'I can't wait,' Ollie said.

'We won't let you down,' Sophia told her.

'I know,' Kim said.

Sophia and Ollie headed back inside where Pixie and Ollie's dad were waiting for them.

'Soph, your mum had to go back to the Hospital,' Max said. 'She'll meet you later, but I think this calls for a celebration. I'm on break so how about ice creams all round? My shout!'

Ollie's smile faded. 'As long as it's not soft serve,' he muttered.

'Oh, Ollie!' Pixie slung her arm around his shoulders. 'Don't be a party pooper.'

Ollie sighed. 'Enough with the poo jokes,' he said. But Sophia could see he was smiling, just a little.

Ice creams in hand, they made their way to one of the harbour-view lawns to enjoy the afternoon sun.

To Ollie's horror, Sophia had chosen chocolate. He'd stuck to his new favourite, vanilla.

'What the –' Ollie exclaimed, as

something large and wet fell from the sky. He lifted his hand.

'Don't –' Sophia started, but then she could only shake her head and giggle.

Slowly Ollie took his hat off. There, right on the crown of his favourite Taronga cap was a big white bird poo.

Sophia's shoulders were shaking. She pointed at his hat. 'I guess you found some vanilla-coloured poo,' she squeaked.

Ollie looked from the poo on his hat to his ice cream. He rolled his eyes and sighed.

Sophia took a breath, calming her giggles. 'It could have been worse,' she said.

'How?' Ollie asked.

'Imagine what would have happened if you weren't wearing your hat!'

Ollie tilted his head as he looked at Sophia. 'Very true.'

He put his hat back on his head with a grin and had a big lick of ice cream.

Sophia was still laughing as she turned to look out over Sydney Harbour. It was a perfect blue-sky day and the sun was making the sea sparkle.

She wanted to capture this feeling and hold it forever.

For the first time in her life, she knew there was nothing she'd rather be doing and no place she'd rather be.

Ollie's FUN fact file

- Capybaras do two different types of poop. One is hard and brown - they don't eat that one. The other one is soft and green and still has lots of nutrients in it.
- Bat poo can be sparkly if they eat insects with an exoskeleton made from a shiny substance call 'chitin'.
- Hyena poo is sometimes white because they chew and swallow bones.
- Most poo is roundish, but wombat poo is shaped like cubes. That's because their intestines have ridges that squeeze it into a square shape.
- When threatened, opossums don't run away. They lie down and do a poop

that smells like rotting flesh. Predators think they're already dead and leave them alone.

- Some beetle larvae eat leaves that are poisonous to other animals and then cover themselves with their own poo to make themselves toxic. It's called a 'faecal shield'.
- Some fancy coffee is made from coffee beans collected from the poo of a palm civit. And elephant poo can be turned into paper.
- There are whole beaches made from the poo of parrotfish. They eat the algae off coral, but can't digest the coral so they poop it out.
- Baby pandas, hippos and elephants all eat their mum's poo – but koala mums produce a special kind of poo called 'pap'. It's filled with useful bacteria.

TARONGA
CONSERVATION SOCIETY AUSTRALIA®

For the Wild

This book has the power to protect.

This series was created in partnership with Taronga Conservation Society Australia. Taronga is a not-for-profit organisation whose vision is to secure a shared future for wildlife and people.

Taronga has released more than 55,000 animals into the wild through its conservation breeding programs and rehabilitation at its two Wildlife Hospitals and contributes to more than sixty conservation programs, including seventeen recovery breeding programs.

So when you purchase this book, visit their two Zoos, stay overnight, donate, or participate in an unforgettable behind-the-scenes experience, you're saving wildlife and supporting critical conservation work here in Australia and around the world.

Thank you for being a supporter for the wild.

taronga.org.au

About the author and illustrator

Kristin Darell is the acclaimed author of the Football Fever series with Football Australia. She has also worked as a journalist for major Australian news organisations and is the Program Manager for the Australian Children's Laureate Foundation. She lives on Sydney's northern beaches with her husband, two children, two dogs, pet snake and three-legged pygmy bearded dragon.

Laura Wood is originally from a small town in the north of Italy. She studied illustration in Melbourne, where she started her illustration career. She works in both commercial art and books for children. After a few years of travelling around the world, she now lives in Milan, Italy.